WHAT IS GOLF?

WRITTEN AND ILLUSTRATED BY ANTHONY RAVIELLI
ATHENEUM/SMI, NEW YORK, 1976

Library of Congress Cataloging in Publication Data

Ravielli, Anthony.
What is golf?

SUMMARY: Traces the history of golf emphasizing its
evolution as an international recreation and explains
the techniques and strategy of the game with
suggestions for improving both.
1. Golf-Juvenile literature. [1. Golf]
I. Title.
GV965.R27   796.352'3   75-38342
ISBN 0-689-30518-4

Copyright Text and Illustrations © 1976 by Anthony Ravielli
All rights reserved
Published simultaneously in Canada by McClelland & Stewart, Ltd.
Manufactured in the United States of America
First Edition

To Georgia, Jane, Ellen and
"Zoopy," a happy foursome

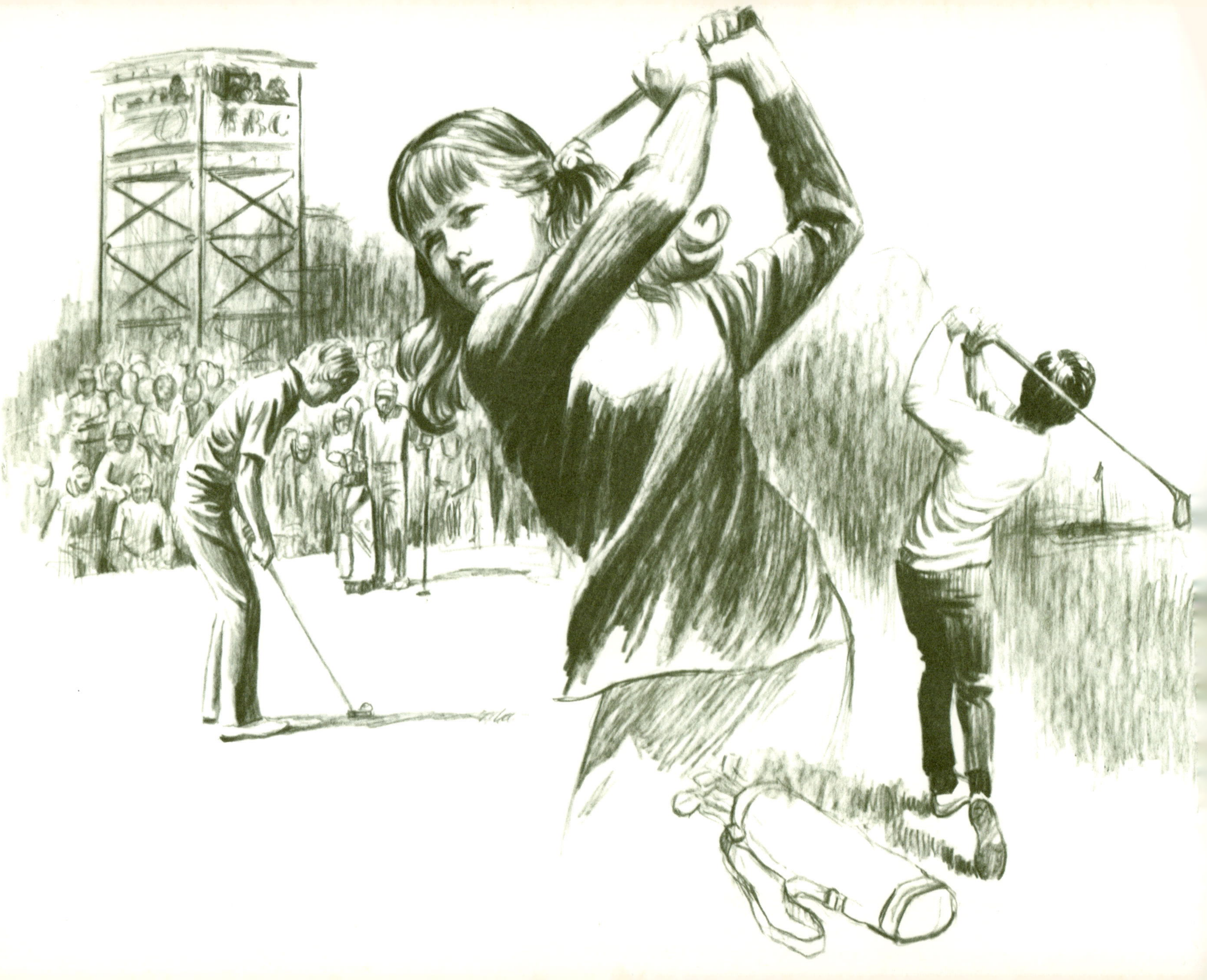

Golf is probably the most popular of all outdoor participant sports. It is played throughout the world by more than twenty million people of all ages—men, women, boys and girls.

Golf is also one of our biggest spectator sports. Thousands of fans attend tournaments to watch famous golfers compete for prizes, while countless others follow the big tournaments at home on television.

But did you ever wonder how a game like golf came into being? Where it originated? And why it attracts so many to its fold?

The story of golf is a mixture of legend and fact—the game of golf, a challenging test of physical skill and mental control.

Let us examine both.

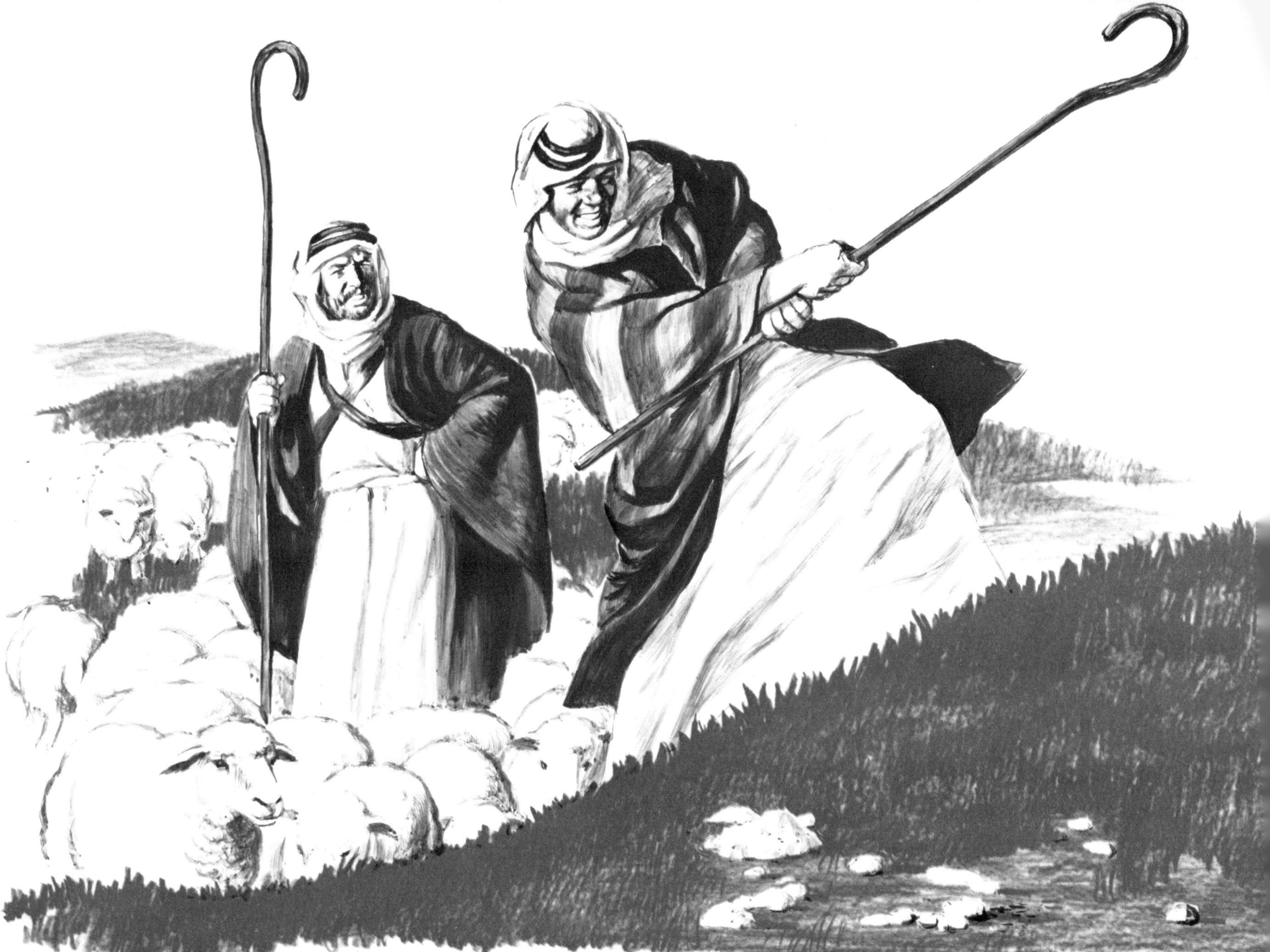

Scholars who study the game claim that Scotland is the birthplace of golf. They point to written records which attest to the fact that the Scots, 500 years ago, played a game in which a variety of clubs were used to hit a ball over the countryside and into a hole dug in the ground.

Yet, many historians are of the opinion that striking a ball with a club, or a stick, is such a natural act that some sort of golf must have been played long before the Scots are supposed to have invented the game.

Although they have no written proof, these same historians theorize that perhaps the cradle of golf could have been a hillside pasture on an ancient Mediterranean island, thousands of years ago. A weary shepherd, to break the monotony of tending sheep, may have swung his crook at large, round pebbles. He may have aimed at distant targets and one day the pebble may have hit a target and rolled into a nearby hole. He was probably thrilled by his achievement, and so tried it again and again. When he mastered the shot, he might have taken the first step that led to the sport by challenging other shepherds to duplicate his feat. At least, that is how some historians believe golf began.

The shepherd's game is, of course, a fable. We will never know if it is true. But it could have happened, because we do know that stick-and-ball games, of one kind or another, existed more than two thousand years ago in some Mediterranean countries, including ancient Rome.

In 100 B.C., for example, the Romans played a game called paganica which bore a curious resemblance to golf. Paganica was played on a field a few hundred yards in length. Upright posts at each end of the field served as goals. The players, wielding thick, L-shaped branches as clubs, tried to propel a skin-covered ball stuffed with feathers across the field and against the post of the opposing team.

We don't know if the Romans observed any rules or, for that matter, counted their strokes, but a case can be made for paganica as an ancestor of golf. It contained the elements from which a variety of games evolved.

The Roman Legions, as they spread over Europe, played their games in every country they occupied. Which may explain why an abundance of stick-and-ball games, all offshoots of paganica, appeared in so many European countries at about the same time.

One such game, called *jeu de mail,* developed in France; another, called *chole,* evolved in Belgium; *cambuca* took hold in Britain; and *het kolven* emerged in Holland.

To play jeu de mail, the French used a small wooden ball and a mallet with a long, springy shaft. The "fairway" was usually a wide highway lined with rows of hedges which provided a natural boundary to the narrow "course." A pole was raised a few hundred paces down the highway. Players took turns trying to hit the pole in the least number of strokes.

Jeu de mail produced its quota of big hitters. Tall tales were told of their herculean efforts. Drives of more than four hundred paces were reported. Expert golfers of today who have tried hitting a replica of the wooden ball with those ancient mallets think the reports were somewhat exaggerated. Or, as one scholar put it, "were there gigantic drivers in those days, or only gigantic liars?"

The Belgium game of chole and the British game of cambuca were similar to jeu de mail, which was simply an extension of paganica. But het kolven, as played in Holland around the sixteenth century, looked very much like golf—at least, in pictures.

Paintings and drawings made by Dutch artists during that period show men and children holding and swinging what appear to be golf clubs. One drawing shows four people on a grassy field with a player in the act of "putting." His form, to say the least, seems peculiar, but there is no doubt as to what he is doing. These scenes obviously show the game of het kolven being played on the land in the summertime. Other drawings depict the Dutch playing the same game in the wintertime on their frozen canals.

The historians who favor Holland as the launching pad of modern golf—on the strength of the drawings—would have us believe that golf was imported to Scotland from Holland. Either by Scottish sailors who, shipwrecked off the Netherlands, were taught the game by their rescuers. Or, by Scottish merchants who traded with Holland and brought back clubs and feather balls which, at that time, were not manufactured in Scotland.

Neither of these stories are documented. As a matter of fact, the Dutch eventually lost interest in playing het kolven outdoors and converted it into an indoor game totally unlike golf.

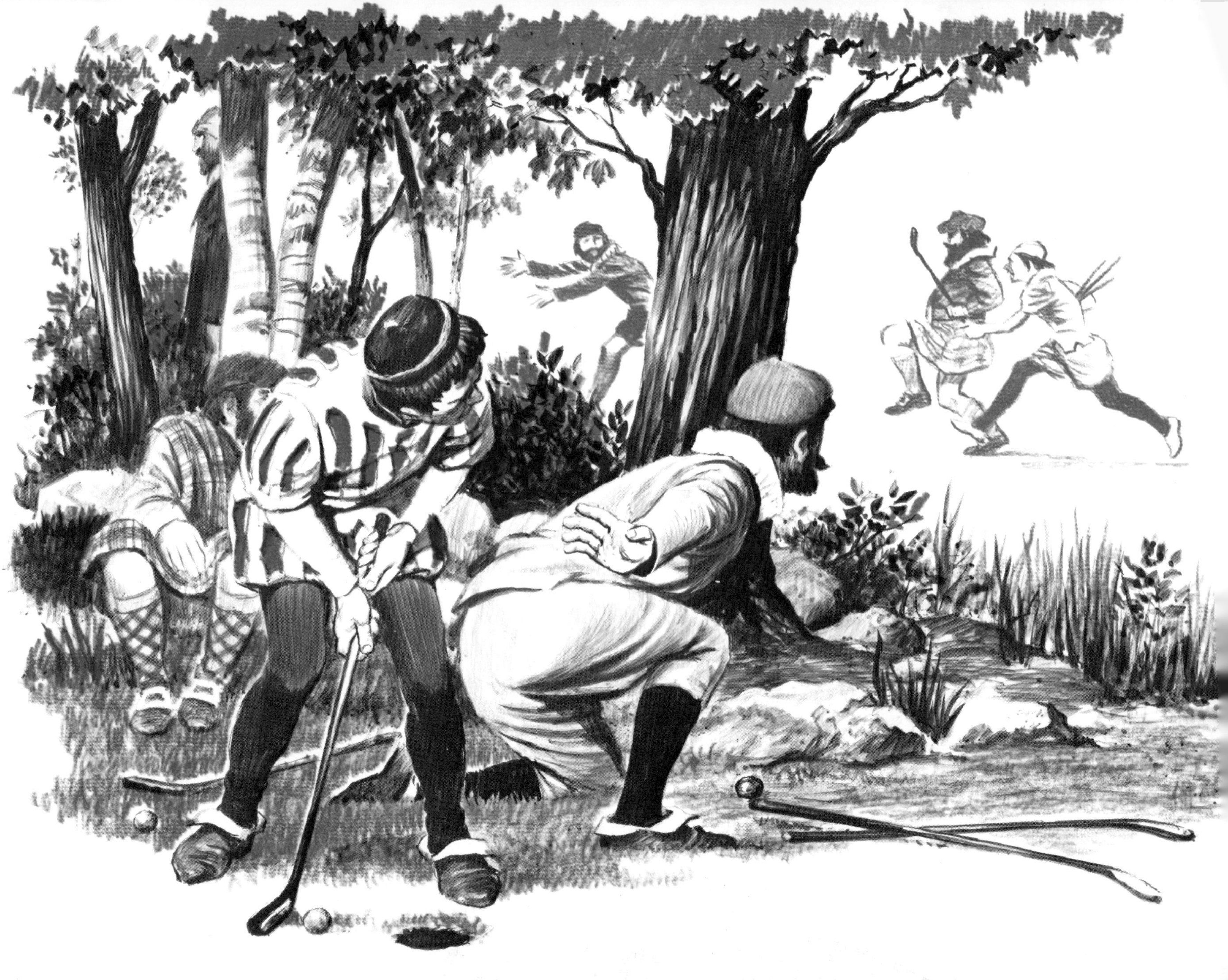

"Kolf" is from a Danish word meaning club, and the Dutch referred to het kolven as a "kolf" game. The feather-stuffed ball that was used to play het kolven was called a "kolf" ball. Perhaps the Scots adopted the word when they imported the "featheries" for their game from Holland. But that is where the similarity between the Dutch game and the Scottish game ends.

Golf as we know it today is strictly a Scottish game which may or may not have evolved from paganica but which, by the fifteenth century, had already become one of Scotland's national sports. It was so widely played in 1457 that the Scottish Parliament, at the insistence of King James II, issued an edict forbidding the playing of "Fute-ball and Golfe" because they interfered with the practice of archery, which was needed for national defence.

Despite the efforts of three successive monarchs to banish the game, golf continued to flourish in Scotland behind the sheriff's back. In fact, by the sixteenth century the Scottish people were so preoccupied with the game that church attendance fell off. Concerned church officials, alarmed by the situation, forbade the playing of "golfe" on Sundays. But, even though violators were hunted down and punished, neither the state nor the church succeeded in suppressing the game.

For generations, golf remained one of the few recreations enjoyed by the common people of Scotland. During the sixteenth century it became the favorite pastime of Scottish royalty as well. Even James IV, whose laws made the game illegal, was bitten by the golf bug.

His successor, James V, an avid golfer himself, passed his love for the game on to his daughter Mary, Queen of Scots, who has the honor of being the first woman golfer in history.

It isn't surprising that Mary's son, James VI, was born with golf in his blood. He was so addicted to the sport that he surrounded himself with a golfing court, a personal clubmaker, and an official ballmaker to avoid paying the outrageously high prices of imported "kolf" balls.

Charles I, who ascended the throne in the early seventeenth century, continued in the royal tradition and spent much of his reign on golf courses. According to history books, he was in the middle of a golf match when news of the Irish Rebellion reached him.

Needless to say, when the ancient game of golf became royal, restrictions lessened. For one thing, the invention of gunpowder had made archery obsolete. And for another, the rulers themselves were as involved in the game as the people they were trying to restrict. So, in 1633, Charles I lifted all bans imposed on golfers by church and state.

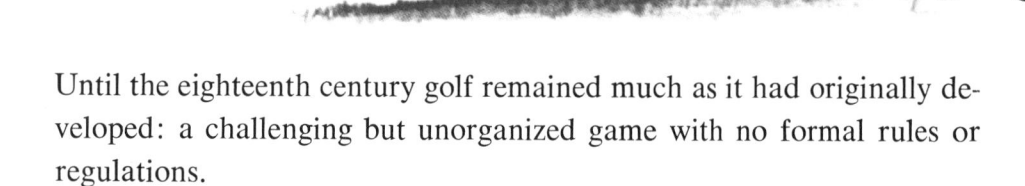

Until the eighteenth century golf remained much as it had originally developed: a challenging but unorganized game with no formal rules or regulations.

Then, in 1744, an attempt was made to bring order to the game. First, a group known as the Honourable Company of Edinburgh Golfers made up a list of thirteen rules for their local tournaments. And then, ten years later, another group of dedicated golfers organized the St. Andrews Society of Golfers, which eventually came to be known as the Royal and Ancient Golf Club of St. Andrews.

Because of its famous Old Course, where their game has been played longer than anywhere in the world, St. Andrews is a shrine for all golfers. But its importance goes beyond that. By expanding the original thirteen rules into a strict code of play that was observed by all golfers, the Royal and Ancient club became the game's governing body.

The R and A rules accompanied the game wherever it spread: to England in the 1850s, where golf boomed into instant popularity. And then across the ocean in the 1880s when golf began to trickle into the United States and Canada.

Golf in the New World got off to a slow start. It was played occasionally by English immigrants during the seventeenth and eighteenth centuries, and then seemed to disappear from the scene. Not until the tail end of the nineteenth century did golf begin to reappear in the United States. Barely a handful of men played the game in 1885 when the first golf club was formed in Foxburgh, Pennsylvania. And only slightly more joined the ranks when the venerated St. Andrews Golf Club of Yonkers, New York was founded in 1888.

During the following few years, the game was practically ignored by the general population, but those it did attract were enthusiastic and influential people. They formed clubs and built courses in many eastern states, and some as far west as Illinois. As the number of golfers increased, tournaments were held and supervision was needed.

In 1895, with the help of the Royal and Ancient Golf Club of St. Andrews, Scotland, the United States Golf Association was organized. The U.S.G.A. serves the same function in America as the R and A serves in Great Britain—to promote and police the game. All golfing nations today observe their jointly-formed rules.

Under the watchful eyes of the U.S.G.A., golf in America became a well-regulated though little known sport until 1904, when a self-taught golfer named Walter J. Travis made national headlines by becoming the first American to win the British Amateur Championship. But it wasn't until 1913 that the popularity of golf began to skyrocket in this country. That was the year when Francis Ouimet, a twenty-year-old former caddy from Boston, won the U.S. Open by beating two of England's greatest golfers, Harry Vardon and Ted Ray.

WALTER J. TRAVIS

HARRY VARDON

TED RAY

FRANCIS OUIMET

In the years that followed, America produced some of the finest men and women golfers in the world. Among the most famous is the immortal Bobby Jones, who dominated the game from the early 1920s to 1930 and is considered the greatest amateur golfer that ever lived. Jones shared the spotlight with the fabulous Water Hagen—the top professional of his day. In recent times, other giants have appeared on the scene. The names of Ben Hogan, Patty Berg, Arnold Palmer, Mickey Wright and Jack Nicklaus are familiar to everyone.

Today, golf has grown to gigantic proportions, not only in the United States but all over the world. It is played in over one hundred and fifty countries, and on all kinds of terrain—on seaside links, on inland meadows, on plains, in deserts and over mountainsides.

Golf is unlike most other games in that the field, or *course,* on which it is played is of no set size. Some courses vary in length by more than a thousand yards, although most are between 6,000 and 7,000 yards long.

A golf course consists of either nine or eighteen *holes.* Each hole starts with a *teeing area* where the ball is placed on a wooden peg, or *tee,* to be hit toward the *putting green*—a closely mowed plot of ground where the hole, or *cup,* is located. Between the teeing area and the putting green is the *fairway*—a stretch of land that resembles a well-kept lawn.

Fairways are of no standard length, width or shape. They can be long or short, wide or narrow, straight or curved, level or undulating. They are usually bordered by *rough* such as tall grass, trees, bushes, or dense woods. Other challenges that surround or cut into fairways are referred to as *hazards.* The most common hazards are ponds, streams, *bunkers* (often called sandtraps), and, on seaside links, the ocean itself.

Golf equipment must conform to strict U.S.G.A. specifications. This includes the size and weight, and even the velocity, of the ball. Clubs are also made to meet U.S.G.A. specifications and, according to the rules, golfers are limited to fourteen clubs when playing a round of golf.

Clubs are carried in a *golf bag* which is a container especially built for the purpose. The majority of golfers wear spiked shoes to secure their footing when swinging the club, but younger players may wear sneakers or rubber-soled shoes.

Over the years, equipment has undergone drastic changes. The feather-stuffed ball, which was used for centuries, was replaced in 1847 by a ball made of solid, latex gutta-percha, which in turn was made obsolete in 1902 by the wound rubber ball of today.

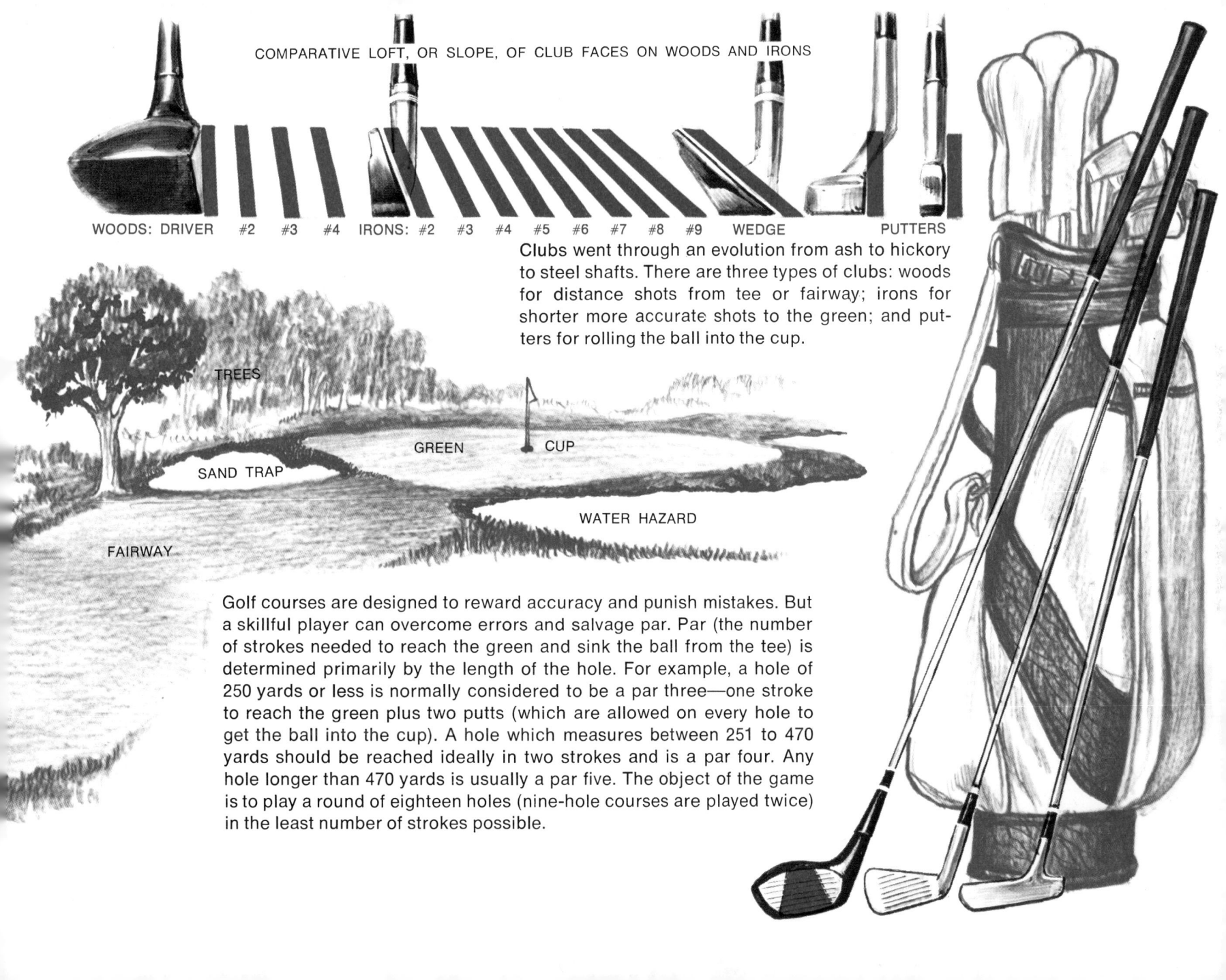

COMPARATIVE LOFT, OR SLOPE, OF CLUB FACES ON WOODS AND IRONS

WOODS: DRIVER   #2   #3   #4   IRONS: #2   #3   #4   #5   #6   #7   #8   #9   WEDGE   PUTTERS

Clubs went through an evolution from ash to hickory to steel shafts. There are three types of clubs: woods for distance shots from tee or fairway; irons for shorter more accurate shots to the green; and putters for rolling the ball into the cup.

TREES

GREEN   CUP

SAND TRAP

WATER HAZARD

FAIRWAY

Golf courses are designed to reward accuracy and punish mistakes. But a skillful player can overcome errors and salvage par. Par (the number of strokes needed to reach the green and sink the ball from the tee) is determined primarily by the length of the hole. For example, a hole of 250 yards or less is normally considered to be a par three—one stroke to reach the green plus two putts (which are allowed on every hole to get the ball into the cup). A hole which measures between 251 to 470 yards should be reached ideally in two strokes and is a par four. Any hole longer than 470 yards is usually a par five. The object of the game is to play a round of eighteen holes (nine-hole courses are played twice) in the least number of strokes possible.

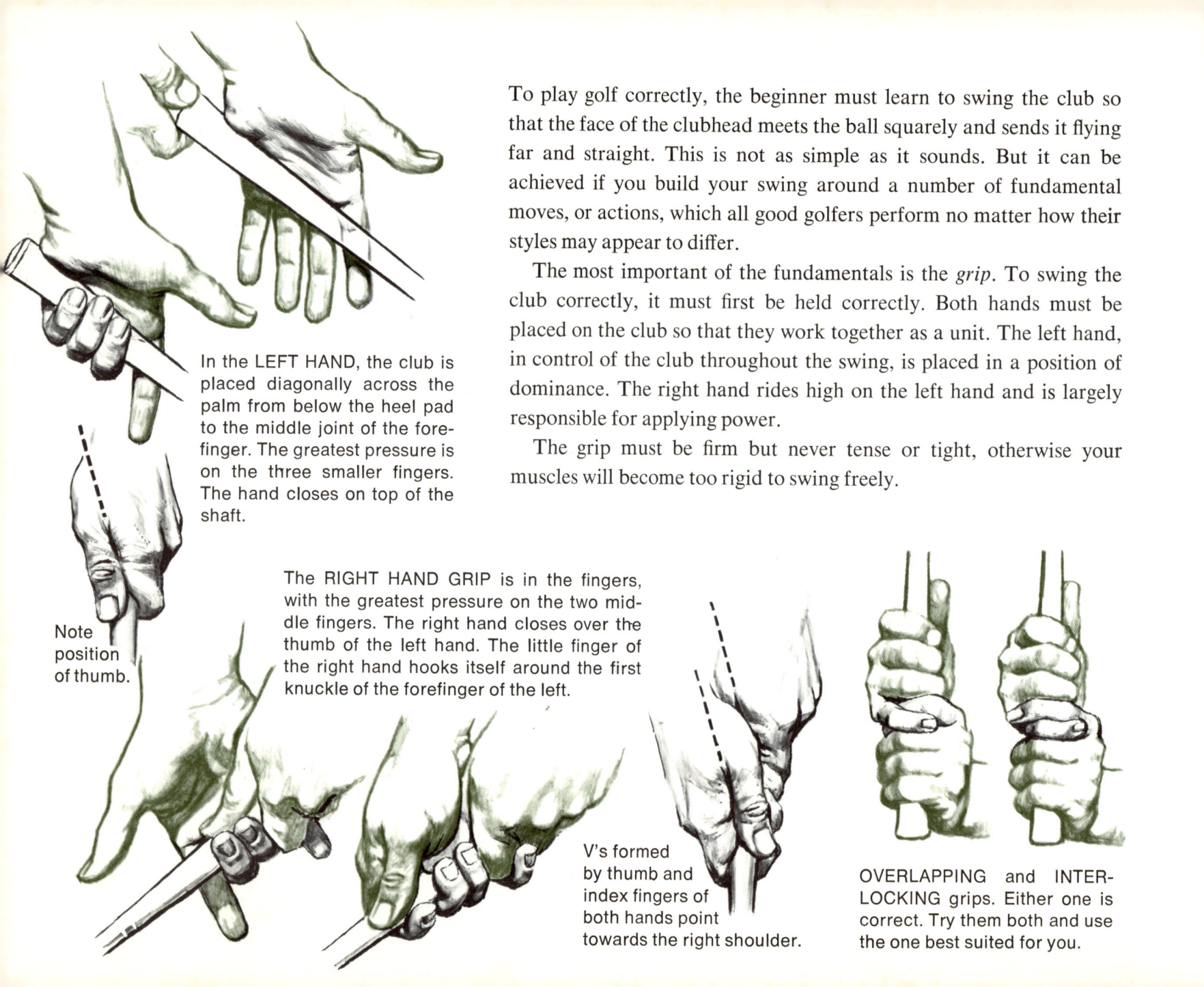

To play golf correctly, the beginner must learn to swing the club so that the face of the clubhead meets the ball squarely and sends it flying far and straight. This is not as simple as it sounds. But it can be achieved if you build your swing around a number of fundamental moves, or actions, which all good golfers perform no matter how their styles may appear to differ.

The most important of the fundamentals is the *grip*. To swing the club correctly, it must first be held correctly. Both hands must be placed on the club so that they work together as a unit. The left hand, in control of the club throughout the swing, is placed in a position of dominance. The right hand rides high on the left hand and is largely responsible for applying power.

The grip must be firm but never tense or tight, otherwise your muscles will become too rigid to swing freely.

In the LEFT HAND, the club is placed diagonally across the palm from below the heel pad to the middle joint of the forefinger. The greatest pressure is on the three smaller fingers. The hand closes on top of the shaft.

Note position of thumb.

The RIGHT HAND GRIP is in the fingers, with the greatest pressure on the two middle fingers. The right hand closes over the thumb of the left hand. The little finger of the right hand hooks itself around the first knuckle of the forefinger of the left.

V's formed by thumb and index fingers of both hands point towards the right shoulder.

OVERLAPPING and INTERLOCKING grips. Either one is correct. Try them both and use the one best suited for you.

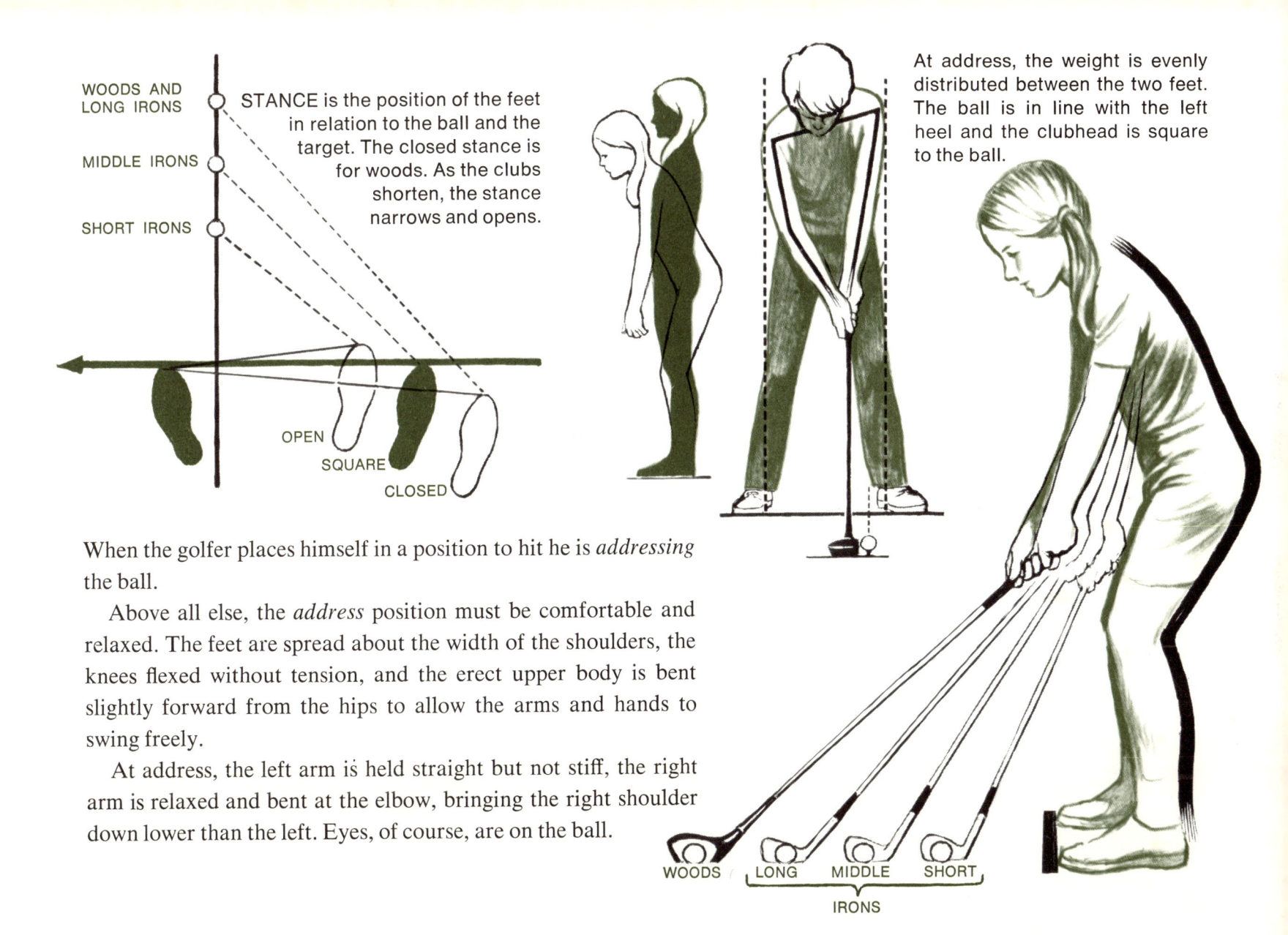

STANCE is the position of the feet in relation to the ball and the target. The closed stance is for woods. As the clubs shorten, the stance narrows and opens.

At address, the weight is evenly distributed between the two feet. The ball is in line with the left heel and the clubhead is square to the ball.

When the golfer places himself in a position to hit he is *addressing* the ball.

Above all else, the *address* position must be comfortable and relaxed. The feet are spread about the width of the shoulders, the knees flexed without tension, and the erect upper body is bent slightly forward from the hips to allow the arms and hands to swing freely.

At address, the left arm is held straight but not stiff, the right arm is relaxed and bent at the elbow, bringing the right shoulder down lower than the left. Eyes, of course, are on the ball.

The position at address is relatively the same for all clubs, but the position of the ball and arms is determined by the length of the shafts of the various clubs.

Fig. 1. *Fig. 2.* *Fig. 3.*

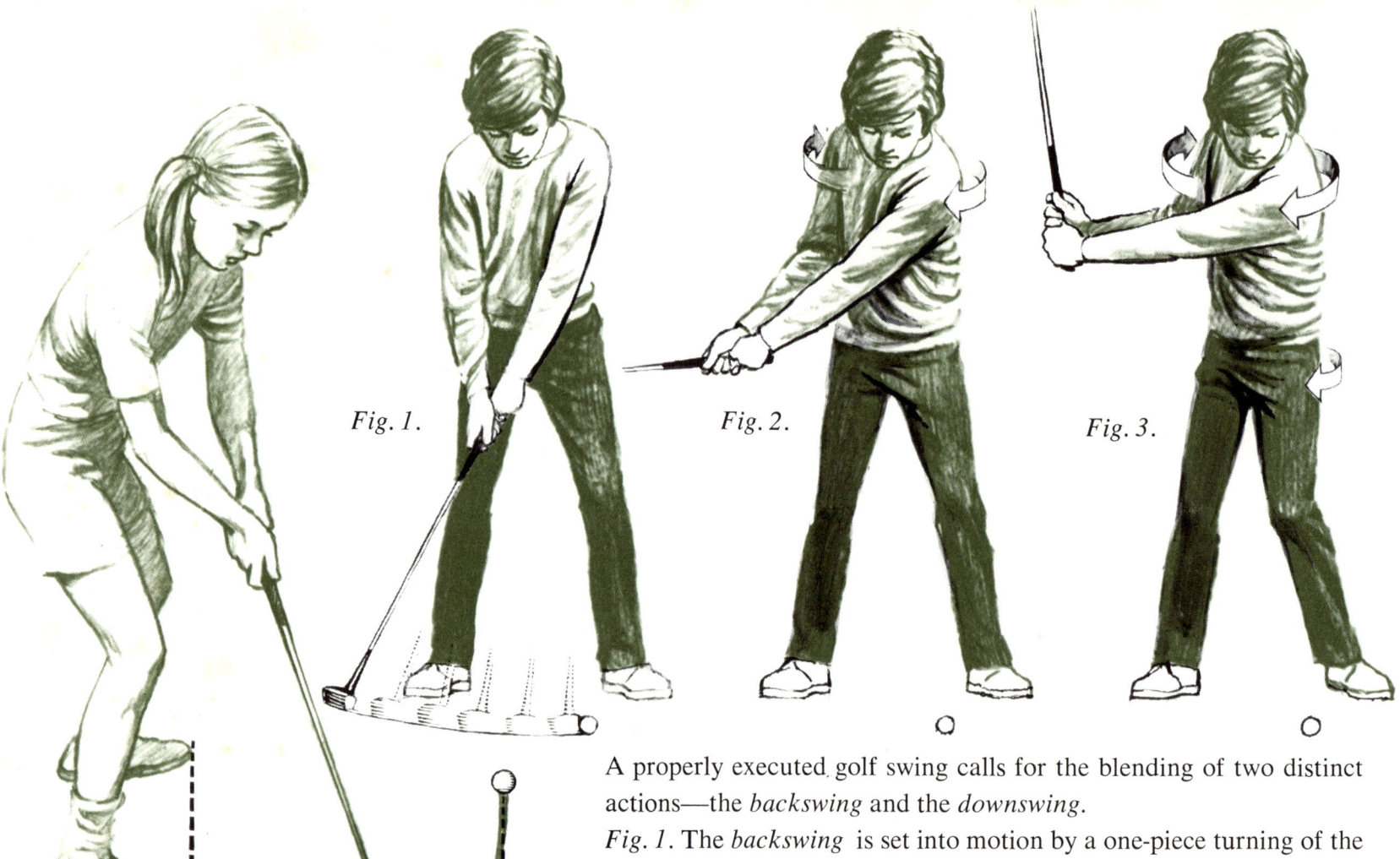

Take your clubhead away from the ball slowly; straight back for a few inches and then, gradually, inside the target line while moving it up and around your body.

A properly executed golf swing calls for the blending of two distinct actions—the *backswing* and the *downswing*.

Fig. 1. The *backswing* is set into motion by a one-piece turning of the shoulders, arms, hands and club, just as the spokes of a wheel move with the hub. The left arm and club form an unbroken line. This action starts the clubhead straight back away from the ball along the target line close to the ground and puts it on its proper "track."

Fig. 2. As the backswing continues, the head remains fixed, the shoulders turn around the spine and the left arm stays straight.

Fig. 4.

At the top of the swing, the left hand will be in firm control of the club, the right hand relaxed and the wrists cocked naturally by the momentum of the moving clubhead.

In the completed backswing, the left shoulder is under the chin. The left arm and the back of the left hand form a straight line. The hands and club are behind and higher than the head. The club points towards the hole.

Fig. 3. At about the halfway mark, the hands come into play and cock the wrists just enough to help bring the clubhead up. By now the swing is starting to pull the hips around, and the weight, equally distributed at address, flows toward the right foot.

Fig. 4. At the top of the backswing the shoulders and hips have turned as much as they can. Most of the weight is on the right foot, and the left heel has been pulled off the ground slightly by the rotating hips. The left knee has not dipped forward, but has bent inward toward the right knee.

A straight left arm and a full shoulder turn around a fixed axis (the spine) make it possible to swing the club in a wide arc and repeat it in the same groove time after time.

As the downswing begins, return the elbow of the right arm back to the side of the body.

Fig. 5.

Fig. 6.

Fig. 5. Start the *downswing* by *turning the left hip* towards its original address position. This early hip turn forces the left heel to the ground, transfers the weight from the right leg to the left where it belongs when hitting, and brings the arms down to within hitting range.

Fig. 6. The shoulders, arms and hands lag behind the hips at the start of the downswing, but they gradually gather speed as they enter the hitting zone. At this point, the right elbow is close to the side, the left arm is straight, the left hand is firm, but the right hand is relaxed and cocked, ready to unleash its power.

THE DOWNSWING IS TRIGGERED BY TURNING THE LEFT HIP TOWARDS THE HOLE

Fig. 7.

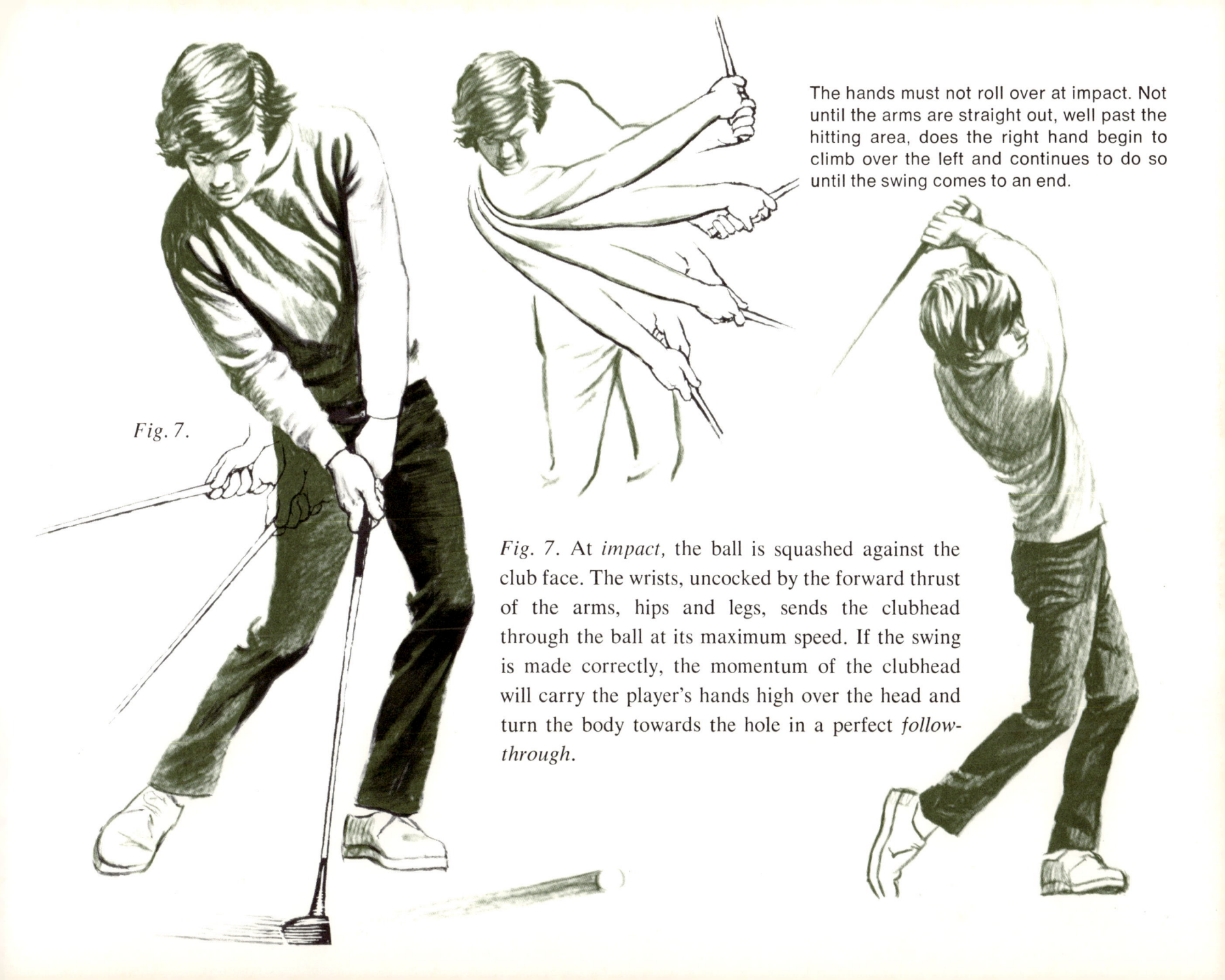

The hands must not roll over at impact. Not until the arms are straight out, well past the hitting area, does the right hand begin to climb over the left and continues to do so until the swing comes to an end.

Fig. 7. At *impact,* the ball is squashed against the club face. The wrists, uncocked by the forward thrust of the arms, hips and legs, sends the clubhead through the ball at its maximum speed. If the swing is made correctly, the momentum of the clubhead will carry the player's hands high over the head and turn the body towards the hole in a perfect *follow-through*.

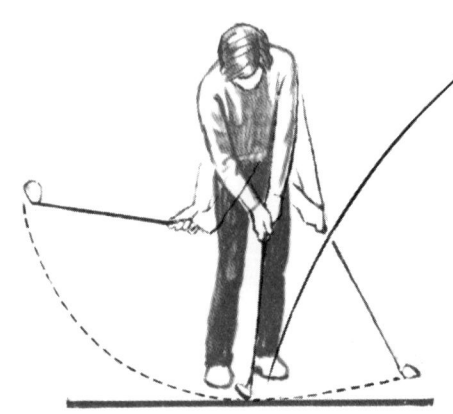

A PITCH SHOT is made with a minimum of body action. The weight shifts to the left foot early on the downswing. The wrists become straight and firm at impact and follow-through.

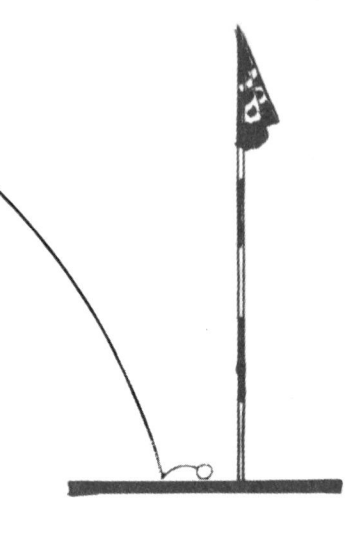

PITCHING AND CHIPPING

The *pitch* and the *chip* are short, delicate shots made to the green.

A *pitch* is a high shot with very little roll. It is used to fly the ball over rough ground or some other obstacle and land it softly near the hole. A 9 iron or wedge is used. The stance is open and narrow, the left arm is straight, the hands are close to the body, and the head remains fixed. The club is taken back with the left arm and hands, the wrists cock early, and the backswing is short.

A normal *chip* flies low, lands just on the green and runs toward—hopefully into—the hole. For a chip, a 6, 7, or 8 iron is frequently used. The feet are close together, the stance is very open and the hips are turned slightly towards the hole. There is practically no body action for this shot. The weight stays on the left side throughout the swing.

A CHIP SHOT is made with the arms and hands, there is little or no wrist break. The backswing and follow-through are kept low.

Fig. 1.

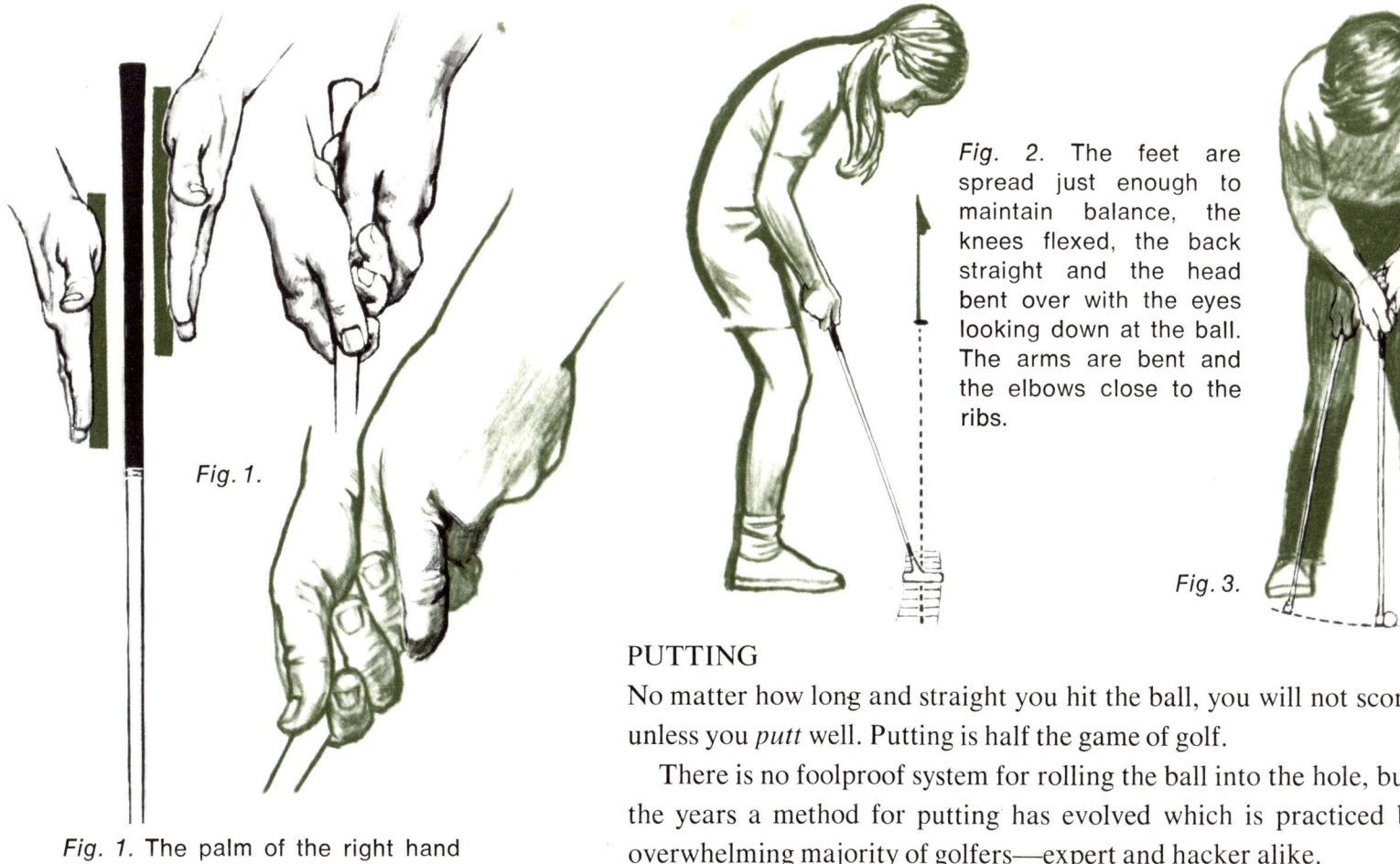

Fig. 2. The feet are spread just enough to maintain balance, the knees flexed, the back straight and the head bent over with the eyes looking down at the ball. The arms are bent and the elbows close to the ribs.

Fig. 3.

Fig. 1. The palm of the right hand and the back of the left hand face the hole. The club is gripped in the palm and fingers of both hands with the forefinger of the left hand riding over the fingers of the right. Both thumbs are on top of the shaft.

PUTTING

No matter how long and straight you hit the ball, you will not score well unless you *putt* well. Putting is half the game of golf.

There is no foolproof system for rolling the ball into the hole, but over the years a method for putting has evolved which is practiced by the overwhelming majority of golfers—expert and hacker alike.

The club is held with a *reverse overlap grip* (*Fig. 1*)

The posture is *relaxed* but compact (*Fig. 2*)

The putting stroke is made with the *arms* and *hands*, keeping the putter low to the ground going back and coming through (*Fig. 3*)

There must be no swaying of the body during the stroke and the head must remain perfectly still at all times. Study the green, visualize an imaginary line from the ball to the cup and stroke the putt along that line.

DO'S AND DON'TS

- When taking the grip, place the clubhead behind the ball SQUARE TO THE TARGET LINE. A closed or open club face at address, even if the grip, backswing and downswing are perfect, will result, at best, in a hook or slice at impact.

- At address, don't stand too far from the ball. REACHING will force you to bend too sharply at the waist, stiffen your legs, put you off balance and restrict your swing—a combination of faults which are bound to produce a bad shot.

- Don't pick the club up with your hands on the takeaway. Start the backswing ALL IN ONE PIECE by turning the shoulders, arms, hands and club slowly at the same time.

- DON'T BE IN A HURRY TO HIT THE BALL! Start the downswing by UNWINDING THE HIPS first. Haste will cause you to hit from the top, uncock your wrists too soon, prevent you from shifting your weight to the left foot, bring you outside the target line and—if you hit the ball at all—will produce a weak slice or a topped shot.

- And above all, be sure you DON'T SWAY. Keep your head fixed throughout the swing. Even though there is body action leading to impact, the triangle formed by the head and feet at address must be maintained until after the ball has been hit.